ANGEL PIG
& THE HIDDEN CHRISTMAS

ANGEL PIG
& THE HIDDEN CHRISTMAS

JAN L. WALDRON
pictures by DAVID MCPHAIL

PUFFIN BOOKS

To my mother, for memorable Christmases,
and for Samantha, with love   J.L.W.

For Jan—with thanks and admiration for turning
my single note into a symphony   D.M.

PUFFIN BOOKS
Published by the Penguin Group
Penguin Putnam Books for Young Readers, 345 Hudson Street, New York, New York 10014, U.S.A.
Penguin Books Ltd, 27 Wrights Lane, London W8 5TZ, England
Penguin Books Australia Ltd, Ringwood, Victoria, Australia
Penguin Books Canada Ltd, 10 Alcorn Avenue, Toronto, Ontario, Canada M4V 3B2
Penguin Books (N.Z.) Ltd, 182-190 Wairau Road, Auckland 10, New Zealand
Penguin Books Ltd, Registered Offices: Harmondsworth, Middlesex, England

First published in the United States of America by Dutton Children's Books, a division of Penguin Books USA Inc., 1997
Published by Puffin Books, a division of Penguin Putnam Books for Young Readers, 2000

1 3 5 7 9 10 8 6 4 2

THE LIBRARY OF CONGRESS HAS CATALOGED THE DUTTON EDITION AS FOLLOWS:
Waldron, Jan L.
Angel Pig and the hidden Christmas / by Jan L. Waldron; illustrated by David McPhail.—1st ed.   p.   cm.
Summary: A group of pigs discover the meaning of Christmas.
ISBN 0-525-45744-5 (hardcover)
(1. Christmas—Fiction. 2. Pigs—Fiction. 3. Stories in rhyme.) I. McPhail, David M., ill. II. Title.
PZ8.3.W1485An 1997 [E]—dc21 96-37646 CIP AC

Puffin Books ISBN 0-14-056591-4

Printed in the United States of America

'Tis the day before Christmas, the house is a-flutter.
The pigs are abuzz cleaning up all the clutter.
They're sweeping and washing and waxing the floors.
They're dusting the bookshelves and polishing doors.

They hike to the attic, up seven steep flights,
To look for the candles, the wreaths, and the lights.
But the balls are in pieces, the tinsel is tangled,
Their stockings have holes, and their old tree is mangled.

So the piggies assemble a long Christmas list.
They check it again to see what they've missed.
And when they are ready, they trudge through the snow—
But the one with the wallet is knee-deep in woe.

"We don't have the money to buy any gifts.
We're fresh out of cash—no *buts*, *ands*, or *ifs*.
We'll have to miss out on this once-a-year day.
We haven't the credit or incoming pay."

"We used to have savings." "Oh, where did they go?"
"We spent them, I guess." "On what?" "I don't know!"
"We forgot to remember that Christmas was near,
And now the Big Day is about to be here!!!"

The pigs were despondent, some started to bawl.
"*Now* we can't go to the outlets and mall
   To buy jeans and sneakers with fancy brand names,
   And TVs and CDs and video games."

They checked every pocket, without much success.
They dug for lost quarters, they made a big mess.
Christmas seemed finished before it began.
The pigs had no money, no hope of a plan.

As the piggies sat silent in sadness and gloom,
A mysterious spirit invaded the room.
A glittery mist drifted down from above.
The feeling it brought them was something like love.

"You think you need money? You don't!" said a voice.
"You just need each other and time to rejoice."
The pigs peered around and then up in the air.
An angel pig hovered above the blue chair.

"Christmas means many and various things—
Singing and laughing and green paper rings,
Homemade mint candies and fresh eggnog, too,
Striped shortbread cookies and caramel goo.

"Create your own Christmas from what is right here,
With boxes and crayons and cake-baking gear.
Get out your toolbox, there are toys to be built.
Cut up old clothes, stitch a colorful quilt.

"Giving and sharing and just helping out,
 That is what Christmas is really about.
 Look all around you, that's where you should start.
 You'll find the best giving is done with your heart."

Angel Pig's message was simple and clear:
The magic of Christmas was merrily near.
The pigs dug up paint sets and found colored clay.
They molded a vase and a festive red tray.

They rooted in closets and under beds, too,
Searching for fabric and scissors and glue.
With pipe cleaners, markers, and small shiny stars,
They made pencil holders and fat cookie jars.

They thought up some poems, which they wrote down in books,
Then went to the kitchen and turned into cooks.
They baked gingerbread piggies and macaroon cats,
Butterscotch reindeer and chocolate-chip hats.

As they covered their gifts in potato-print wrapping,
Some of the pigs began dozing and napping.
The rest spied the clock: eleven-oh-three!!!
They had less than an hour to search for a tree!

Everyone scurried, including the mouse,
To go find a tree that would fit in the house.
But when they stepped out in the glistening snow,
They noticed an evergreen brightly aglow.

A tree they had hurried past many a time
Looked suddenly radiant, festive, sublime.
On bushy green branches ice gleamed in the night.
The pigs stood in awe and beheld the new sight.

The cardinals, the blue jays, and even the crows
Trimmed the tree with red berries, with ribbons and bows.
One of the pigs made a bowl of mulled cider
While other pigs caroled and chorused beside her.

"This is a Christmas we'll never forget."
"And it's only begun." "It's not over yet."
"There'll be more songs tomorrow, and gifts and great food
To add to our bountiful holiday mood."

"Good night, get some rest—Happy Christmas to you."
And with that, Angel Pig swiftly vanished from view.
The piggies all beamed and admitted with cheer
The best Christmas of all had been hiding right here.